W9-BYK-766

Foreword

I first met Maynard Moose one foggy morning years ago in downeast Maine. He was sitting on a mossy log, telling stories to a chipmunk and a crow. Pure chance had led me down that path—chance and great good fortune. For I had stumbled upon the last living teller of Mother Moose Tales—those strange and magical stories sent down by Mother Moose herself so long ago.

I visited Maynard many times over the following months, and finally gathered the courage to ask him if I might record his tales for posterity. He readily agreed, and I began to make a series of field recordings, hoping to one day make the stories into books.

When the time came to translate Maynard's tales into print, however, I faced unexpected difficulties. Moose language (even Modern Moose) has its own laws and rhythms, quite different in many ways from human speech. And as you will hear on the enclosed CD, moose do not pronounce words quite the way that we do. The moose substitution of the *th* sound for *s*, for example, made translating Maynard's voice to the page especially challenging. In the end, we decided to humanize Maynard's pronunciation, but to keep the original Moose vocabulary intact. We trust the glossary will make Maynard's meanings clear. When reading aloud, those unfamiliar with the cadences of moose speech will find the field recording a useful guide.

May all humans discover, and discover once more, the joys of gathering together to hear the old tales told again.

—Willy Claflin

the little Moose who couldn't go to sleep

A Maynard Moose Tale
As told to Willy Claflin

Illustrated by James Stimson

AUGUST HOUSE
Little folk

For Jacqueline, my dearly beloved insomniac.
　　　　　　　– W.C.

For Willy, Jacqueline, and Maynard, for always
including me in their adventures.
　　　　　　　– J.S.

For Little Moose, her very self.
　　　　　　　– M.M.

WARNING
THIS BOOK CONTAINS MOOSE GRAMMAR,
SPELLING, AND USAGE,
ALL OF WHICH HAS BEEN KNOWN TO
SCRUMBLE UP THE HUMAN BRAIN.

Book design by Graham Anthony
Guest edits by Jacqueline Darrigand
Audio CD recording, music, and
voice-over introduction by Brian Claflin

Printed by Pacom Korea
Seoul, South Korea
December 2013

10 9 8 7 6 5 4 3 2 1

LIBRARY OF CONGRESS CATALOGING-IN-PUBLICATION DATA

Claflin, Willy, 1944-
 The little moose who couldn't go to sleep : a Maynard Moose tale / as told to Willy Claflin ; illustrated
by James Stimson.
    pages cm
 Summary: Little Moose learns the value of a good night's sleep.
 ISBN 978-1-939160-67-6 (alk. paper)
[1. Moose--Fiction. 2. Sleep--Fiction.] I. Stimson, James, illustrator. II. Title. III. Title: Little moose who
could not go to sleep.
 PZ7.C52155Li 2014
 [E]--dc23
　　　　　　　　　　　　　2013013601

The paper used in this publication meets the minimum requirements of the American National Standard
for Information Sciences—Permanence of Paper for Printed Library Materials, ANSI Z39.48-1984.

　　　　　　　　　AUGUST HOUSE, INC.
　　　　　　　　　　　ATLANTA

Glossary

Moose Words and Their English Equivalents

Note: Although this text has been painstakingly translated from the original Moose, it contains many traces of Piney Woods English, a dialect generally used by Aroostook County Mooses in northern Maine. In the text, Piney Woods words have been designated in **bold**.

Amunal: animal

Bankee: blanket (the favorite one)

Baskies: baskets

Blorble: bubbling musically to oneself

Blumberry: A dark sweet bushberry from the Northern Piney Woods. Eating at least three blumberries a day can help you think in the dark.

Bunk, Bunkle: to clunk and bumble about

Conversatiable: a friendly conversation

Detention: attention

Diagnosticals: extremely grown-up and important medical pontifications

Disorderations: stuff that's wrong with you

D'ow, Phoo!: Never you mind what this means—it is a distremely indappropriate thing to say, especially in school! Bad moose!

Driftee: to slowly drift, mostly side-ways, sometimes upside down

Elephump: elephant, especially a chubby one

Gaddump: to gallop

Gaddunk!: sound mooses make when landing on a rug

Frangleberries: Small orange berries that grow in the shade of the mufflewort tree; sweet and spicy, they cause some to hiccup and sneeze

Pedogogeez: A complex plan of educational instruction formulated by Very Important Mooses for the purpose of imparting information to the young Moose brain

Purpee: purple (the deep bright kind)

Shklork!: the sound made by a moose when turning over in a bathtub full of mashed potatoes

Skimmering: gliding and skipping over anything shimmering

Snork!: inadvertent soporific nasal exclamation

Splooped: bubbling up over the edge of a pot

Splorp!: Sound made by Piney Woods tea being poured into a to-go cup

Sporkle: sparkle most brightly and mysteriously

Tuckee: to tuck in snugly

Far away in the Northern Piney Woods there lives a storyteller named Maynard Moose. Every full moon in the forest, the animals come from far and near to hear him tell the old Mother Moose Tales, handed down so long ago. Young and old, big and small, fur and feather, the woodland creatures gather round and settle down on moss and branch and log to listen.

And when the moon's not full, or there's no moon at all? Then Maynard can often be found telling tales by the bedside of Little Moose, his favorite cousin and youngest of kin.

My mommy used to tell me a nursery rhyme, when I was a little moose. She would say this:

> Mother Moose, Mother Moose, Where Have You Been?
> I been to the kitchen and then back again.
> Mother Moose, Mother Moose, what did you there?
> I make the whole universe out of thin air.

My mommy used to say, "Is one thing to make a universe out of Thick air. But to make a universe out of Thin air, you got to stir and stir and stir."

So the whole universe come from the kitchen of Mother Moose. That's true! Stories come from Mother Moose's kitchen, too. I will tell you one my mommy used to tell to me. It is called: *The Little Moose Who Couldn't Go to Sleep*.

Once upon a time, a long, long time ago, there was a little moose who could not go to sleep at night.

All the brothers and sisters, as soon as they put their little heads down on their little moosie pillow—**Snork!**—they **driftee** off to Sleepland. But this little moose, no sooner did she lay the head down upon the pillow than a idea would come into the brain part—Boing! Boing!—and **bunk** around there all night long. And she could not get to sleep!

And in the morning, when the mommy moose bang on the big saucepan with the big iron spoon—Clang! Clang!— all the brothers and sisters jump up and polish the antlers and file down the hoofs and **gaddump** off to the Moose Academy for to learn Proper Posture and Woodland Skills and How to Count to Three over and over again. (That was as far as moose in the forest could count, long, long ago. They would go "One, two, three," and then "lots" was the only number after that.)

Well, Little Moose, she would always drag along behind. She feel like her got a pillow stuffed between the ears. And the teachers shake their heads. "Little Moose does not pay **detention**. She does not learn good, like the brothers and sisters!"

And Little Moose, she feel bad.

"Listen," say the Mommy Moose, "tonight, when you go to bed, I want you to breathe slow and peacie-ful, OK?"

"OK!" Say Little Moose. Her go to bed that night, **tuckee** the self in, under the little **bankee** with the duckies and the zebras.

"I like my little bankee with the duckie and the zebra!" say Little Moose. "Duckies and Zebras on my bankee—dum-de-dum de-dum.... Huh! I wonder why they have picked duckee and zebra to put on my bankee?

*I mean, you could have a **elephump** and flamingo bankee. That would make a nice bankee—elephump and flamingo bankee...you could have any **amunal** you would like. You could have...you could have banana and tarantula! 'Cause I have heard that tarantula like bananas. I wonder if a banana could like a tarantula? Do you think you would have to be a amunal to like something? Or could a fruit or a vegetable like something? I wonder that.*

Or you could have a vegetable on your bankee. You could have a picture of a eggplant or some corns on the cob! Or a picture of a radish or some mashed potato. But not Real mashed potato, 'cause that would gunk up your bankee. Hard to wash off your bankee....

*Or you know what you could have? You could have a bed that would be like a soft bathtub full of mashed potato... nice warm mashed potato—And when you would turn over at night it would go **shklork**!—like that! In the morning, though, you would have to wash out your fur. And how would you wash your bed-clothes? I mean, your bed-potatoes—how would you wash your bed-potatoes...I mean, what if...?"*

And so her brain go like that all night long!

In the morning, when the mommy moose bang on the big saucepan with the big iron spoon—CLANG! CLANG! CLANG!—all the brothers and sisters jump up and polish the antlers, file down the hoofs and gaddump off to the Moose Academy, for to learn Proper Posture and Woodland Skills and How to Count to Three over and over again. And Little Moose drag along behind, feeling like her got Two pillows stuffed between the ears.

"This is serious!" say the teachers.

"This is Very Serious!" say the principal.

And Little Moose, she come home feeling worser than before.

"Listen," say the daddy, "I think it is time for us to consult Old Moose's Very Big Book of Cures and Ruminations."

And so the daddy moose reach up on the shelf and take down Old Moose's Very Big Book of Cures and Ruminations—OOF! put it on the table—Whump!—blow off the dust—Poof!—and open it up.

"Let's see here......Sleep!...there we go ...'Too much of, too little of, history of....um... er...Oh, here it is: 'According to the wisdom of the ancients, confirmed by modern **diagnosticals**, sleep **disorderations** of the brain part come from improper diet and not go to bed early enough. Remedy, or Cure—see below...Eat big bowl of legumes every evening and go to bed an hour earlier than usual.' There! Simple enough, huh?

"**D'ow, Phoo!**" say Little Moose. "Dumb and stupid! I don't want to go to bed early! I don't want to eat lay-goomes!"

"Now, now," say the Mommy. "That's enough of that. You be a good little moose and do what you're told. And when you go to bed tonight, Please—just try to think about nothing, OK?"

"OK," say Little Moose. "I will think about nothing."

So that night Little Moose eat a big bowl of legumes.

"BLUCK!" She go to bed an hour early. "DUMB AND STUPID!" And she try to think about nothing.

"Let's see. I will close my eyes," say Little Moose, "and I will think about nothing.... There—that is a nice kind of nothing—is all darkness! With just some little orange sparkles. And there is sort of a **purpee** *blob over there, and a green blob over there.... That's a very nice nothing, with a purpee blob and a green blob and some little orange sparkles!*

Dum-de-dum...But that could not be really Nothing. 'Cause for it to be Nothing, there would have to be no sparkles or blobs!

For to be nothing there would have to be no darkness neither! You would have to take away the darkness and the blobs and the sparkles. And also you would have to take away me, and take away the house, and....

Ooo-ooo!—you would have to take the sky out of the sky, and the forest out of the forest.... You would have to take everything in the universe out of the universe....

And then you would have to put it somewhere! You could not call That nothing—it would just be moving everything over one big space! You could not call That nothing....

Maybe once upon a time there was nothing; maybe there was nothing before there was anything. Maybe before Mother Moose, maybe.... But then where would Mother Moose have come from? You cannot have something come from nothing....

Maybe she came from a big Moose Egg!

But now that would be the opposite of nothing, because then Mother Moose and everything in the universe would have come out of the Moose Egg, and.... That would be Everything! That would not be Nothing, because for it to be...."

And so her brain go like that all night long!

And in the morning, when the mommy moose bang on the saucepan with the big iron spoon – CLANG! CLANG! CLANG! – all the brothers and sisters jump up, polish the antlers and file down the hoofs, and Gaddump! Gaddump! off they go to the Moose Academy, for to learn Proper Posture and Woodland Skills and How to Count to Three over and over and over again. And Little Moose drag along behind, like her got a whole mattress stuffed between the ears.

"This is serious!" say the teachers.

"This is Very Serious!" say the principal.

"This is Bad!" say the superintendent. "We will have to have a Parent Conference! Little Moose does not pay detention!"

"Dow, Phoo!" say Little Moose.

"Hmmm!" say the Principal. "Saying Phoo! in school. Big Black Mark on your record!"

"Oh dear, oh dear," say Little Moose. Her drag along home, feeling worser than before.

"Listen, Little Moose," say the Mommy. "Tonight when you go to bed, I have a idea. How about counting sheep? I have heard that counting sheep is a good way to go to sleep."

"OK," say Little Moose.

So she eat the big bowl of legumes. "BLUCK!"

She go to bed an hour early. "DUMB AND STUPID!"

And she start to count sheep.

"One, two, three..."

"Maaaahh!" *Dingy-ding*! (They have a little bell around the neck.)

"One, two, three..."

"Maaaahh!" *Dingy-ding*!!

"One, two, three..."

"Maaaahh!" *Dingy-ding*!

"Oooo—look! I have go one, two, three the First time. I have go one, two, three the Two time! I go one, two, three the Three time. That make three threes! That makes a little box of three sheeps! Three on top, three in the middle, three on the bottom, and three on the side. And three from corner to corner! It is a box of threes!

"Ooo—look! If I do two More boxes of three's, then I will have three boxes! And if I do three more boxes and then three more boxes, then I will have a big box of boxes! A big box of boxes of threes!

"Ooo—that was fun! Let's do that again! One, two, three..."

"Maaahhh!" *Dingy-ding*!

"One, two, three...."

"Maaaahh!" *Dingy-ding*!

"One....... Two......."

And just as she was about to driftee off to sleep...

Suddenly the second sheep say: "Good evening!!"

"Oh, no!" say Little Moose. "No! No! Who are you?"

"I am the second sheep," say the second sheep. "You know who I am—you have counted me!"

"No, but why do you Speak with me?" say Little Moose.

"Well, you speak with me; I speak with you—that makes for a **conversatiable**," say the sheep. "Maybe you do not want to speak with me. Maybe you do not like sheep."

"No, no, no," say Little Moose. "You are supposed to put me to Sleep!"

"Oh!" say the sheep. "A sheep put a moose to sleep? That would be a big job—for a sheep to put to sleep a whole moose! How about just the nose and the foot part?"

"No, no, no—it is the Brain part," say Little Moose. "Put the Brain part to sleep!" "Oh," say the sheep, "the Brain part...Well, um...let's see—how would I do that?

"Um...Oooo! I know! Some tea! Maybe some tea! Would you like some nice warm slurpy tea from the kitchen of Mother Moose?"

"Oh yes!" say Little Moose. "Some tea would be nice. But the kitchen of Mother Moose—what is that?"

"That is where Mother Moose make everything in the Universe," say the sheep. "Duckies and zebras, pond weed and thunder. Galaxies and tea are her specialties! Would you like to go?"

"Oh yes," say Little Moose, "I would like that very much!"

"Well," say the sheep. "Look out the window. See that star? The bright one? Well, that is not really a star, Little Moose. It is the front porch light of Mother Moose's Kitchen, far off in the sky. No more questions, now. Climb on my back and hang on tight, and off we go."

"OK," say Little Moose.

Swoosh! Out the window they go: up and up into the dark night sky, where the warm winds blow and the stars all **sporkle** and blink.

"Ooo, look," say Little Moose, "The star is getting brighter! It is not a star at all!"

And sure enough—so it was not! It was the front porch light of Mother Moose's kitchen, just like the second sheep have said it was.

"Ooo, look!" say Little Moose. "It is like a little cottage, floating in the sky!"

And closer and closer, until **Gaddunk**! They land on the porch, right in the middle of the big welcome mat.

"Hop off and follow me," say the sheep. And he push the door wide open and they walk right in.

Little Moose look around. The little cottage was all one kitchen. There was a pair of antlers on the wall by the door, with coats and caps and jackets and hats and one ginormous umbrella. In the middle of the kitchen was a big woodstove with a kettle and a big black pot that **splooped** and **blorbled** in a most musical manner.

A table and two chairs stood by the window. And the walls were covered with shelves and shelves of bottles and boxes and books and **baskies**, stones and bones and spools of string, jars of nails and jars of candy, jars of marbles and **blumberry** jam. There was everything you can imagine, and several things you cannot. And on the windowsill, fresh from the oven, was a gingerbread moose, set there to cool.

"But where is Mother Moose?" say Little Moose.

"Oh," say the sheep, "it is her night out—she is far away, planting some planets.... Ah, there is the tea, on the shelf by the table!"

Sure enough, high on a shelf by the side of the table were rows and rows of tins of tea, every color of the rainbow.

"Let's see," said the Sheep, "Here is tonight's menu: 'Our selections include a choice variety of foreign and domestic herbal brews' Let's see, um...

"We have Tropical Fandango, Polar Ecstasy, Tundra Supreme, Twilight Misery (I myself do not recommend the Twilight Misery), Redwood Bliss, and Piney Woods Delight."

"I would like the Piney Woods Delight," say Little Moose.

"Good choice," say the Sheep. "It's getting late, so we should get this to go. OK, put the tea in the teacup, dum-de-dum... pour in the water," "**Splorp!**" "Hold on tight, and away we go!"

And swoosh!— down and away they go, through the stars and sparkly darkness, down and down until finally they were once again **skimmering** along above the tops of the trees.

"OK," say the Sheep, "almost home—duck your head and in we go!"

So Little Moose duck her head, and in they swoosh, landing—gaddunk!—on the little rug right by the bed.

"Into bed now," say the sheep, "and slurp real slow."

"OK," say Little Moose. And she climb back into bed.

Slurp! "Oh, boy, this is good teas!" Hmmm...Slurp! "Hmmm...tastes like **frangleberries**..." Slurp! "...Ohmmm...tastes like willow bark and pinecones...and...pondweed...and...nice...Mother Moose tea...."

SNORK!

And slowly she driftee off to sleep, all snug in the bed and warm in the tummy.

Well, the next morning, when the Mommy Moose bang on the big saucepan with the big iron spoon—CLANG! CLANG! CLANG!—all the brothers and sisters jump up and polish the antlers and file down the hoofs, and Little Moose, having had a good night sleep, she jump up, too!

And she put on some nice purple hoof polish and Gaddump off happily to the Moose Academy. And she pay good detention to Proper Posture and Woodland Skills. And she Count to Three over and over again, even better than the brothers and sisters!

And at the Parent Conference, the teachers and principal say:

"Mr. and Mrs. Moose, we are pleased to say that we have finally succeeded in imparting our educational **Pedogogeez**!" (That means, we have teached her real good. We have done a real good job, and are very proud of her.)

So that night, Little Moose do not have to go to bed early. She get to stay up late. "Dum-de-dum!"

And no more lay-goomes! Her get to eat fern lasagna with the brothers and sisters. "YUM!"

And when she tuckee the self in, under the bankee with the duckies and the zebras, she driftee right off to sleep.

And from that time on, whenever she cannot fall asleep, she would count up until the third time second sheep would come along and say,

"Good evening."

And then off they would go, to Mother Moose's Kitchen, to get a cup of tea.

Did Little Moose ever meet Mother Moose Herself? I don't really know. What do you think?

That is the kind of question that can **bunkle** around inside your brain and keep you awake all night long. But if that should happen to you, just call for the second sheep. And maybe he will take you to her kitchen, and who knows? She might even be there, stirring that big pot on the stove; the pot that all stories come from.

Nighty night!

Maaahhh! Dingy-ding!